SEA
of
SURPRISES

Library of Congress Control Number: 2019915914

ISBN: 978-1-950943-02-9

First Printing: October 2019

Illustrations: Cindy Schlaudecker

Interior Design: 102nd Place, LLC, Cave Creek, AZ

SEA
of
SURPRISES

Caren Cantrell

Illustrated by
Cindy Schlaudecker

For our
Granddaughter

May your days be filled
with happy surprises!

Vienna sat twitching her tail in the middle of her favorite tide pool. When would Mr. Pelican arrive? Her best mer-buddy, Chloe, swam up.

"Watcha doin, Vienna? Shouldn't you be getting ready for your birthday party?"

"Oh, I've got all clams of time," Vienna said. "Mer-gran is sending me a surprise from the Seventh Sea. I wish she could be here too."

"Bubblegram for Ms. Vienna of the First Sea,"
squawked Mr. Pelican.
"This doesn't look like much of a surprise," Vienna said.
"Read it," said Chloe.

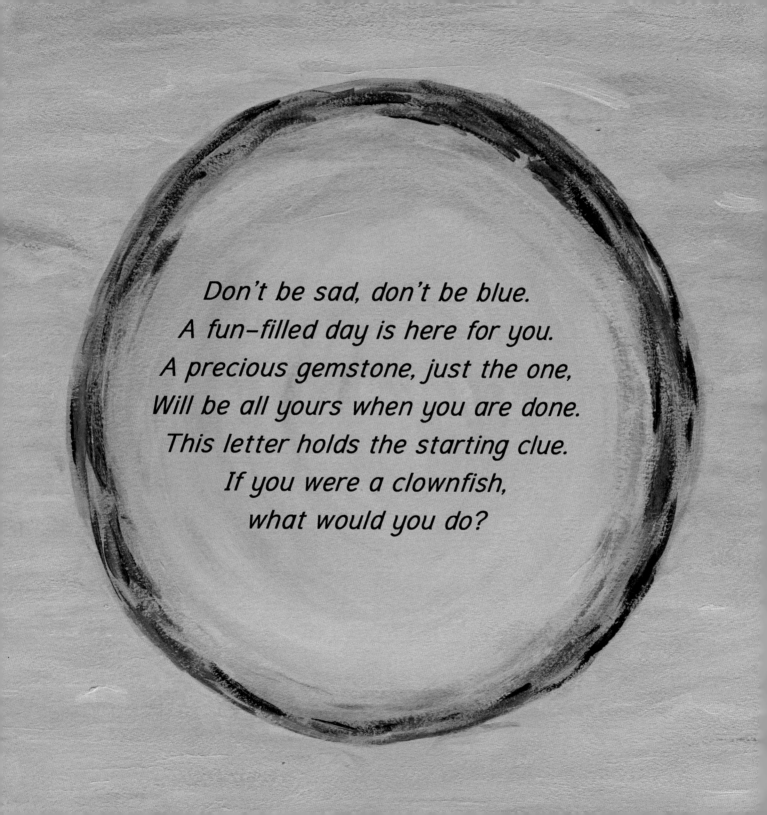

Don't be sad, don't be blue.
A fun–filled day is here for you.
A precious gemstone, just the one,
Will be all yours when you are done.
This letter holds the starting clue.
If you were a clownfish,
what would you do?

"Cool! It's a treasure hunt. Can I help?" Chloe cried.
"Sure, said Vienna, "but what would a clownfish do?"
Chloe replied, "Charlie's always clowning in the coral reef.
Let's go there."

They spied Charlie playing hide and seek with his buddies.
"Hey, Charlie, have you seen any strange bubblegrams
floating around?" asked Vienna.
"Why yes, but you'll have to catch me first!"
He darted into the reef.

Vienna and Chloe raced after him. Charlie was quick
and knew special places to hide.
It took all of their fin-ergy to catch him.
"Now where's that bubblegram?" Vienna asked.

"Right here," said Charlie, lifting
his fin and swishing it over.

*Congratulations!
Here's clue two.
Who loves to leave
an inky goo?*

"Hey, Puffy uses ink on his spikes to tattoo
the sharks," said Chloe.
"He scares me," said Vienna, "are you sure
that's the answer?"

They found Puffy tattooing Whitey. The fish gazed with hungry eyes at the mermaids.
Vienna gulped a deep breath of sea courage and stammered, "Mr. P-p-puffy, d-d-do you have a b-b-bubblegram for me?"

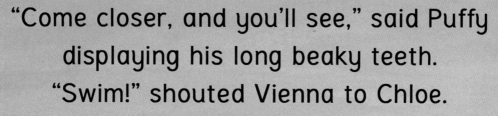

"Come closer, and you'll see," said Puffy
displaying his long beaky teeth.
"Swim!" shouted Vienna to Chloe.

Safe again Vienna said, "I should have known Mer-gran wouldn't send me into danger. I have another idea. Let's call a couple of sea-bers." *Tweet!*
"Take us to Ollie the Octopus," she told the seahorses.

"Ollie, Ollie are you free?" Vienna called.
A dark mist wafted through the water. One long
tentacle appeared, then another, and another.

"I've been expecting you," Ollie hissed. "Check the fourth tentacle on your right."
A rubbery suction cup held a bubble.
Vienna tugged it off and read:

You've done it again!
You're smart as a whip.
Now here's the last clue.
What hides in a ship?

"Treasure!" they yelled.

"Remember the Mermaiden shipwreck we studied in school? That has to be it!"

Vienna shot off using her best dolphin kicks with Chloe right behind.

Vienna gasped when she saw the beautifully decorated ship.

The Crab Street Band played.

All her mer-friends were there.
"Surprise!" they shouted.

Mer-gran swam out of the crowd, a silvery chest in her hand. Vienna's tail wiggled in delight at the sight of her.

"Happy Birthday, my dear," Mer-gran said opening
the chest to reveal a gem of rare Tanzanite.

Vienna gave her gran a huge mer-hug.
"It's beautiful, but Mer-gran, you're the biggest,
best surprise of all!"

More Books by Caren Cantrell

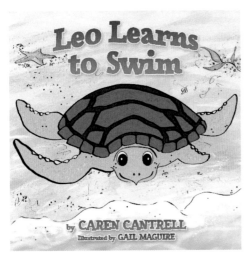

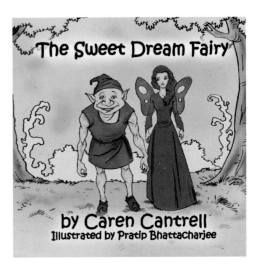

https://carencantrell.com